THIS BOOK BELONGS TO:

____

Presented with love by:

____

On this day:

____

Dear Mom and Dad

Simple Lessons on Love and Life

from Your Child

Dear Mom and Dad

Simple Lessons on Love and Life
from Your Child

Little, Brown and Company
Boston New York London

First Edition

ISBN 0-316-75050-6
LCCN 2001131280

10 9 8 7 6 5 4 3 2 1

WOR

Printed in the United States of America

The text was set in Centaur, and the display type is Goudy Italian Old Style.

Dear Mom and Dad

Simple Lessons on Love and Life
from Your Child

Don't spoil me. I know quite well that I ought not to have all I ask for — I'm only testing you.

Don’t be afraid to be firm with me. I prefer it,
it makes me feel secure.

Don't let me form bad habits. I have to rely on you to detect them in early stages.

Don't make me feel smaller than I am. It only makes me behave stupidly "big."

Don't correct me in front of people if you can help it. I'll take much more notice if you talk quietly with me in private.

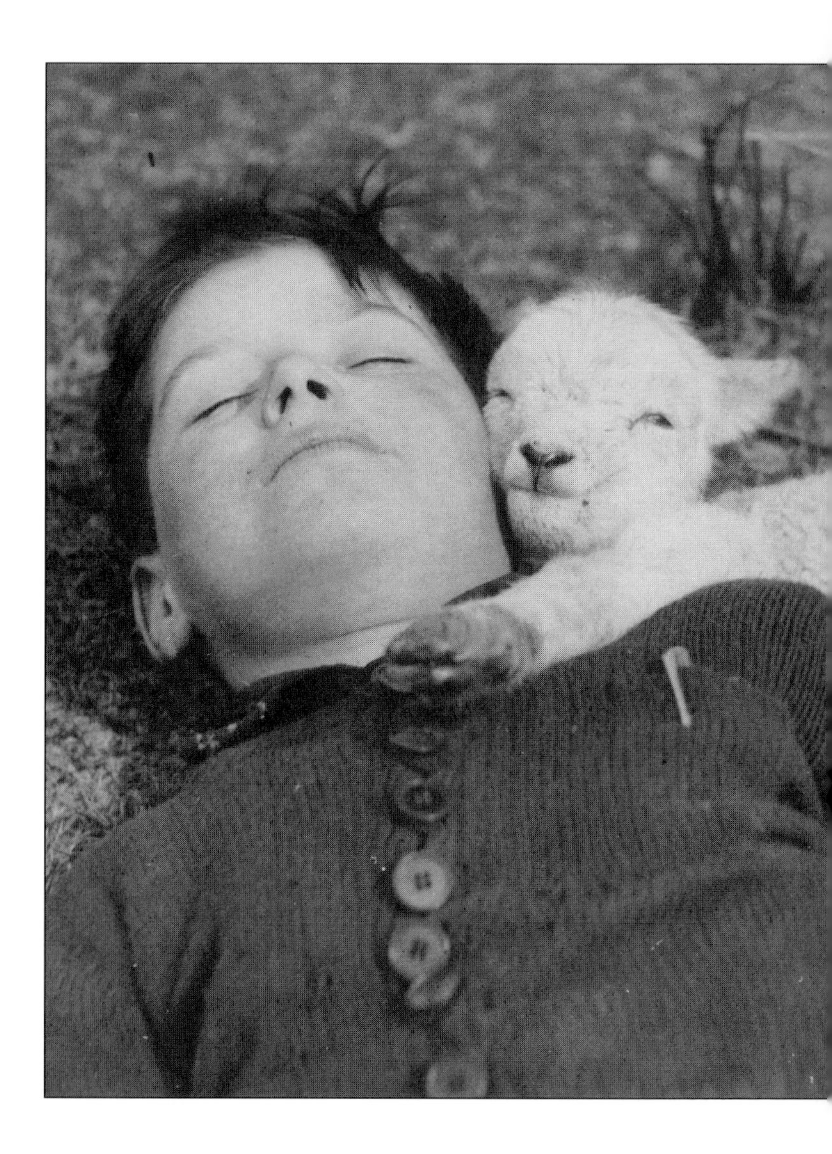

Don't make me feel that my mistakes are sins. It upsets my sense of values.

Don't protect me from consequences. I need to learn the painful way sometimes.

Don't be upset when I say "I hate you." Sometimes it isn't you I hate but your power to thwart me.

Don't take too much notice of my small ailments.
Sometimes they get me the attention I need.

Don't nag. If you do, I shall have to protect myself by appearing deaf.

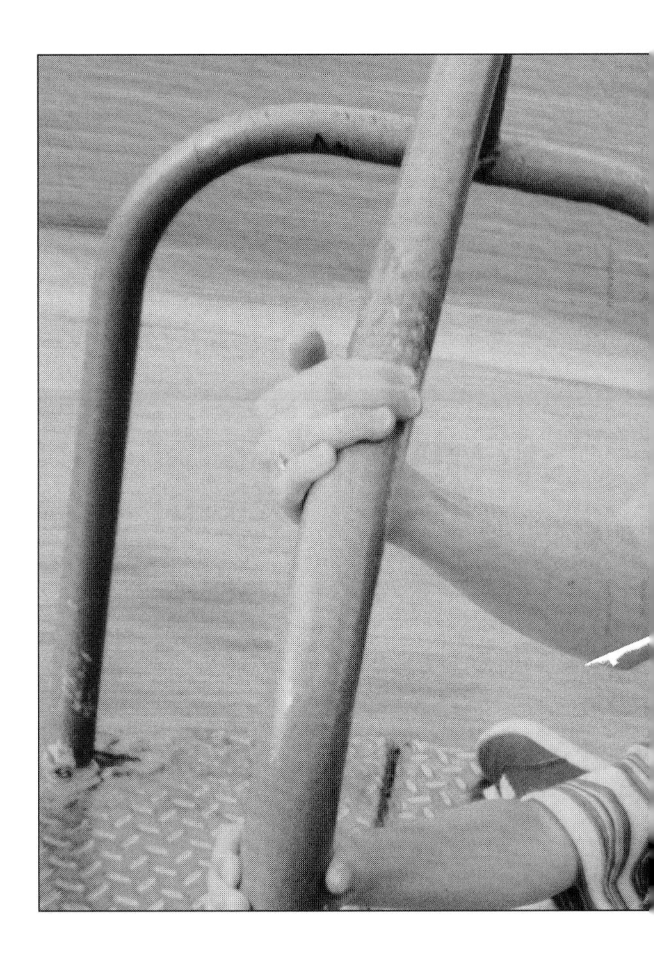

Don't forget that I cannot explain myself as well as I should like. That is why I am not always accurate.

Don't put me off when I ask questions. If you do, you will find that I'll stop asking and I'll seek my information elsewhere.

Don't be inconsistent. That completely confuses me and makes me lose faith in you.

Don't tell me my fears are silly. They are terribly real and you can do much to reassure me if you try to understand.

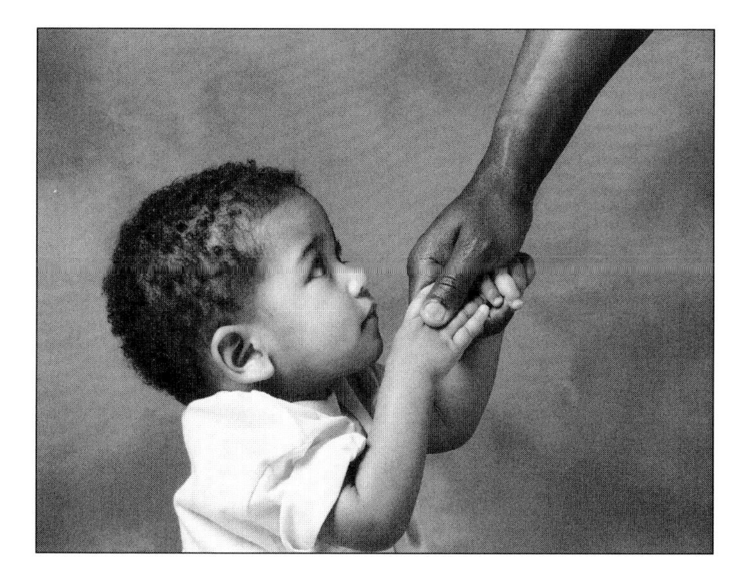

Don't ever suggest that you are perfect or infallible. It gives me too great a shock when I discover that you are neither.

Don't ever think that it is beneath your dignity to apologize to me. An honest apology makes me feel surprisingly warm toward you.

Don’t forget that I love experimenting. I couldn’t get along without it, so please put up with it.

Don't forget how quickly I am growing up. It must be very difficult for you to keep pace with me, but please do try.

Don't forget that I don't thrive without lots of love and understanding, but I don't need to tell you, do I?

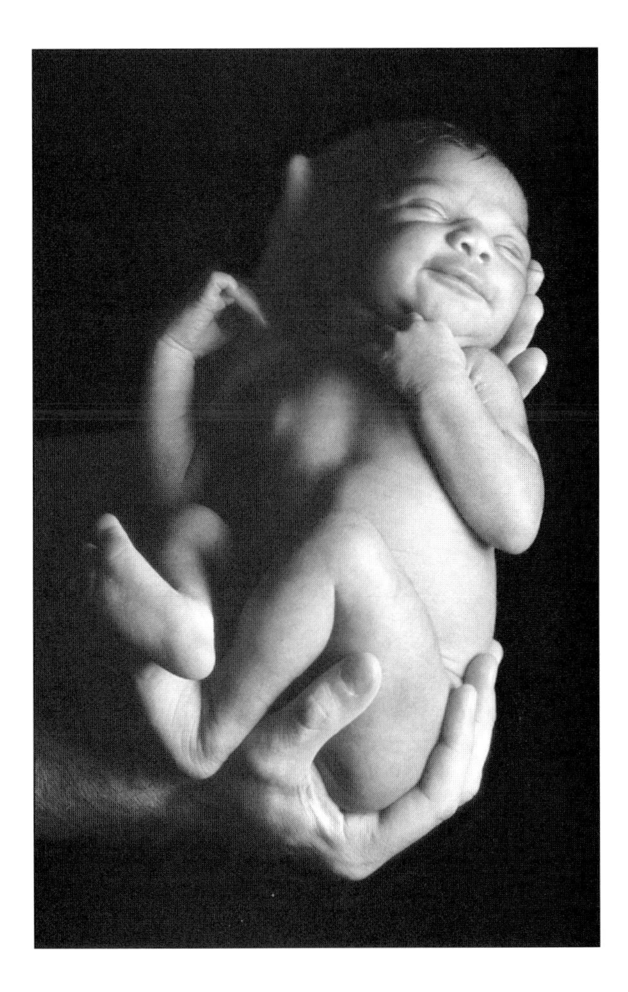

Please keep yourself fit and healthy. I need you.

Photo credits

front jacket: Darren Robb / Stone
title page: Corbis
4: Corbis
7: Corbis
8: Corbis
11: Jamey Stillings / Stone
12: Stuart Redler / Stone
14–15: Hulton Getty / Stone
17: Corbis
18: Corbis
21: Corbis
23: Corbis
24: Terry Vine / Stone
26–27: Stewart Cohen / Stone
28: Corbis
31: Corbis
32: Corbis
35: Corbis
36: Corbis
38–39: FPG International
40: Corbis
43: Corbis
44: Corbis
47: Lori Farr
48: Donna Day / Stone
50–51: Bill Truslow / Stone
back jacket: Peter Cade / Stone